Angel Babies VII

Angel Babies VII
Immortality

Clive Alando Taylor

authorHOUSE

AuthorHouse™ UK
1663 Liberty Drive
Bloomington, IN 47403 USA
www.authorhouse.co.uk
Phone: 0800.197.4150

Published by AuthorHouse 07/05/2016

ISBN: 978-1-5246-3692-0 (sc)
ISBN: 978-1-5246-3693-7 (e)

Angelus Domini
Love Beloved Love

I N S P I R I T* A S P I R E* E S P R I T* I N S P I R E*

Because of the things that have first become proclaimed within the spirit, and then translated in the soul, in order for the body to then become alive and responsive or to aspire, or to be inspired, if only then for the body to become a vessel, or a catalyst, or indeed an instrument of will, with which first the living spirit that gave life to it, along with the merits and the meaning of life, and the instruction and the interpretation of life, is simply to understand that the relationship between the spirit and the soul, are also the one living embodiment with which all things are one, and become connected and interwoven by creating, or causing what we can come to call, or refer to as the essence, or the cradle, or the fabric of life, which is in itself part physical and part spirit.

And so it is, that we are all brought in being, along with this primordial and spiritual birth, and along with this the presence or the origins of the spirit, which is also the fabric and the nurturer of the soul with which the body can be formed, albeit that by human standards, this act of nature however natural, can now take place through the act of procreation or consummation, and so it is with regard to this living spirit that we are also upon our natural and physical birth, given a name and a number, inasmuch that we represent, or become identified by a color, or upon our created formation and distinction of identity, we become recognized by our individuality.

But concerning the Angels, it has always been of an interest to me how their very conception, or existence, or origin from nature and imagination, could have become formed and brought into being, as overtime I have heard several stories of how with the event of the first creation of man, that upon this event, that all the Angels were made to accept and to serve in God's creation of man, and that man was permitted to give command to these Angels in the event of his life, and the trials of his life which were to be mastered, but within this godly decree and narrative, we also see that there was all but one Angel that either disagreed or disapproved with, not only the creation of man, but also with the formation of this covenant between God and man, and that all but one Angel was Satan, who was somewhat displeased with God's creation of man, and in by doing so would not succumb or show respect or demonstrate servility or humility toward man or mankind.

As overtime it was also revealed to me, that with the creation of the Angels, that it was also much to their advantage as it was to ours, for the Angels themselves to adhere to this role and to serve in the best interest of man's endeavors upon the face of the earth, as long as man himself could demonstrate and become of a will and a nature to practice his faith with a spirit, and a soul, and a body that would become attuned to a godly or godlike nature, and in by doing so, and in by believing so, that all of his needs would be met with accordingly.

And so this perspective brings me to question my own faith and ideas about the concept and the ideology of Angels, insomuch so that I needed to address and to explore my own minds revelation, and to investigate that which I was told or at least that which I thought I knew concerning the Angels along with the juxtaposition that if

Satan along with those Angels opposed to serving God's creation of man, and of those that did indeed seek to serve and to favor God's creation and to meet with the merits, and the dreams, and the aspirations of man, that could indeed cause us all to be at the mercy and the subjection of an externally influential and internal spiritual struggle or spiritual warfare, not only with ourselves, but also with our primordial and spiritual identity.

And also because of our own conceptual reasoning and comprehension beyond this event, is that we almost find ourselves astonished into believing that this idea of rights over our mortal souls or being, must have begun or started long ago, or at least long before any of us were even souls inhabiting our physical bodies here as a living presence upon the face of the earth, and such is this constructed dilemma behind our beliefs or identities, or the fact that the names, or the numbers that we have all been given, or that have at least become assigned to us, is simply because of the fact that we have all been born into the physical world.

As even I in my attempts, to try to come to terms with the very idea of how nature and creation could allow so many of us to question this reason of totality, if only for me to present to you the story of the Angel Babies, if only to understand, or to restore if your faith along with mine, back into the realms of mankind and humanity, as I have also come to reflect in my own approach and understanding of this narrative between God and Satan and the Angels, that also in recognizing that they all have the power to influence and to subject us to, as well as to direct mankind and humanity, either to our best or worst possibilities, if only then to challenge our primordial spiritual origin within the confines of our own lifestyles, and practices and beliefs, as if in our own efforts and practices that we are all each and every one of us, in subjection or at least examples and products of both good and bad influences.

Which is also why that in our spiritual nature, that we often call out to these heavenly and external Angelic forces to approach us, and to heal us, and to bless us spiritually, which is, or has to be made to become a necessity, especially when there is a humane need for us to call out for the assistance, and the welfare, and the benefit of our own souls, and our own bodies to be aided or administered too, or indeed for the proper gifts to be bestowed upon us, to empower us in such a way, that we can receive guidance and make affirmations through the proper will and conduct of a satisfactory lesson learnt albeit through this practical application and understanding, if only to attain spiritual and fruitful lives.

As it is simply by recognizing that we are, or at some point or another in our lives, we have always somewhat been open, or subject to the interpretations of spiritual warfare by reason of definition, in that Satan's interpretation of creation is something somewhat of contempt, in that God should do away with, or even destroy creation, but as much as Satan can only prove to tempt, or to provoke God into this reckoning, it is only simply by inadvertently influencing the concepts, or the ideologies of man, that of which whom God has also created to be creators, that man through his trials of life could also be deemed to be seen in Satan's view, that somehow God had failed in this act of creation, and that Satan who is also just an Angel, could somehow convince God of ending creation, as Satan himself cannot, nor does not possess the power to stop or to end creation, which of course is only in the hands of the creator.

And so this brings me back to the Angels, and of those that are in favor of either serving, or saving mankind from his own end and destruction, albeit that we are caught up in a primordial spiritual fight, that we are all engaged in, or by reason of definition born into, and so it is only by our choices that we ultimately pay for our sacrifice, or believe in our rights to life, inasmuch that we are all lifted up to our greatest effort or design, if we can learn to demonstrate and to accept our humanity in a way that regards and reflects our greater desire or need, to be something more than what we choose to believe is only in the hands of God the creator or indeed a spirit in the sky.

It was very much my intention not to state the name of any particular place in the script as I thought that the telling of the story of the Angel Babies is in itself about believing in who you are, and also about facing up to your fears. The Angel Babies is also set loosely in accordance with the foretelling of the Bibles Revelations.

I thought it would be best to take this approach, as the writing of the script is also about the Who, What, Where, When, How and Why scenario that we all often deal with in our ongoing existence. It would also not be fair to myself or to anyone else who has read the Angel Babies to not acknowledge this line of questioning, for instance, who are we? What are we doing here? Where did we come from? And when will our true purpose be known? And how do we fulfil our true potential to better ourselves and others, the point of which are the statements that I am also making in the Angel Babies and about Angels in particular,

Is that if we reach far into our minds we still wonder Where did the Angels come from and what is their place in this world. I know sometimes that we all wish and pray for the miracle of life to reveal itself but the answer to this mystery truly lives within us and around us, I only hope that you will find the Angel Babies an interesting narrative and exciting story as I have had in bringing it to life, after all there could be an Angel Baby being born right now.

After these things I looked and behold a door standing
open in Heaven and the first voice which I heard was like
a (Trumpet!) speaking with me saying come up here and
I will show you things which must take place after this.

Immediately I was in the spirit and behold a throne set in
Heaven and one sat on the throne and he who sat there was
like a Jasper and a Sardius Stone in appearance, And there
was a Rainbow around, In appearance like an Emerald.

Time is neither here or there, it is a time in between time as it is the beginning and yet the end of time. This is a story of the Alpha and the Omega, the first and the last and yet as we enter into this revelation, we begin to witness the birth of the Angel Babies a time of heavenly conception when dying Angels gave birth to Angelic children who were born to represent the order of the new world. The names of these Angel Babies remained unknown but they carried the Seal of their fathers written on their foreheads, and in all it totalled one hundred and forty four thousand Angels and this is the story of one of them.

Angelus Domini

I* M* M* O* R* T* A* L* I* T* Y*VII

When the Angels came to inquire after me, it was only for the asking and inquiring of one simple question, and that question was this, if the prayer had remained the same, as it was always the reality and the case that the examination of my belief and faith of this one peculiar and particular question, was always also the same upon my reply, as I have always spoken out of earnest in replying quite simply Yes, the prayer remains the same.

As even out of the depths of my own mind, I did not know of which amongst the household of these Angels, who would pose to know such an question, for if for some precarious reason I were to be found and to become judged out of my own reason of sanity, to be erroneous in my pleading of these utterances, that indeed I may evoke the wrath of the menace of Beelzebub and indeed the fallen Luciferian devil himself, as I did not stir, but instead retained a state of motionless refrain, as even unto my own mind, I knew in my heart, that Satan would come one way or another to have inflict any sanctions of claim over my right of passage away from this earthly domain towards God's good grace and heavenly kingdom, and so as to be vigilantly aware, that the closer that I became to God, that this would provoke the Devil himself, in tempting me away with mistrust and dissatisfaction, and so therefore I spoke plainly and frankly so as to remind the light of this world of contempt, that the prayers of invocation and that of themselves, no matter who appeared out of the light of the shadows, would quite simply always be and remain the same.

In earnest I attempted to explain, that the prayers of invocation, were simply said in the great piety and humble and respectful nature of appreciation of thankfulness, if only for the simplest truths and tasks of a token and gesture to be met with accordingly, for something of substantial influence that would be deemed faithful in fulfilling the needs of my life as they were presented to me, as the prayers themselves initially and ordinarily came about and had arisen through the circumstances of great loss and regret and sorrow, as also in recognizing the practical and necessary ordinances of worship upon a great platform of reconciliation, that my prayers and hopes and dreams however realized, would become fulfilled within my lifetime, as the prayer itself is a defense and an attribute towards the physical act of prostration in asking and seeking and accepting and receiving the alteration and the exchange, in the form of a bestowment of a redeeming gift placed upon any persons willing to abide and live by its promise, as it also requires the thought and the wit and the meditation, which in itself, can also result in fate through the devotion and dedication and conviction of will and spirit, if the believer is open and truthful and sincere with him or herself, whether we pray for ourselves or for loved ones, or even extensively for something more so.

The prayer remains the one useful objective humane bargaining for the individual that is humble enough in submission, to make such a supplication upon this invocation, as the weight and the gravity and the depth of the intention realized for this purpose when there is nothing else to turn too, which also upon thought, becomes automatically and naturally endowed and sustained with compassion and wisdom and understanding and the paramount realization, in that in some transformative instance, that when we pray for forgiveness, or acceptance, or deliverance, along with the view to enlighten ourselves, and to free ourselves, and to become free from the burden of despair and turmoil, as this is what determines whether such a trial of faith would cause the prayer to become fulfilled.

As for upon the account of God, that Satan would be found to be indefensible, then it would only become befitting that God would judge his servant accordingly, as I recall quite vividly the precious life that I had once lived, and the body that I had once inhabited, but it was upon this new birth of prevailing reality, that for the first seven years of my infancy, that I was always sickly and poorly, due to the fact that I was haunted and tormented by the past of my previous souls existence, for even in the great void and depths of my sorrow and pain, I was recalling and reliving each and every significant moment of a nightmare that took place in the course of events of a lifetime long ago, was I dead, was I alive, was I inbetween worldly places, I truly did not know, even as my Father Nephi could not defend me from the physical struggling of my own demons upon my rebirthing, nor could my Mother Anahita tell me of the things in which she knew not to be of myth and legend but of the truth of a bygone past, but I am Selah, the subdued blessedness of God, coming forth out of my old age and wisdom, and now I am once again in the abundance of my youth, as I was once the fallen desecration of an Earth Mother, given over to death because of my love for a Herald and a General, who held with me great affections and of the highest esteems, in defending and fighting for my heart and in pulling me away from the clutches of another suitor upon the harvest of my destruction, who by divine grace and right is now my father's father.

I am not absolutely sure of where the Angels of my inquisition had arisen from, or from where they fled upon the appointment of Haven the Herald Angel in giving authority and leadership to establish order and prominence in the universal household of magnitude for the hosts of heaven, but with that being mentioned, it is only because the names of the fallen, that have become stricken from the annals of life, and the new heavens have opened up and begun to take shape and form in becoming established, and so therefore the newly elected, have given rise to the new frontier and kingdom of Nejeru.

But as for me and my souls possessions, I now know that I only contain the remnants of the occurrences and the things before, and so now that I am grown by the infinite sum of twenty one summers, I am now fully given back my rights to be an earth mother once again, although I dare not to speak the names of places that had once been fashioned and pronounced in my preexistence of living, but instead I simply watch and wait, and pray and meditate, and succeed to enjoy and partake of the love and the beloved love of my Angelic parents, Anahita and Nephi.

For once I knew and understood more than I could possibly and ultimately account for or even fathom to speak of or against, for my trials within the soul cages had invigorated and reinforced and reinvented me a new and living being, having heard my screams of exhaustion within the terrors and the affliction of scorn upon my very soul, for all of my affection born or endearment in that I had given both life in death and birth unto the exemplary concepts of love unconditional, a child of heaven and earth, now to be removed and rendered invisible from my sight and side, but wherefore and why would God hide and keep from me such a child of mankind, set upon the hierarchy of angels, and where is the beloved that once was him, in that I barely knew and had not yet seen or touched, or even suckled and nurtured from the deepness of his bosom.

But instead held me captive in Sheol, where I was kept in a death lock and a death hold of nothingness, and yet in worship, the chains were loosened by the daring dreams of another, for what can free one can also bring freedom to all, and yet in the grip of the depths, I did swiftly see God instantly transform whilst hiding his abundance inside of me, and yet in so many indescribable ways, I could not explain myself to my own mothers caring and nurturing of me, and in doubt of rectitude, and I to be accursed and sentenced to live this dream now this nightmare again and again, do the ages forever and forever repeat their history time and time again, or am I to atone for each merit of sacrifice unto Lord, or does heaven speak to me with a new address, and a new voice of reasoning in my conviction of commitment, as I wonder, as I wander and dwell within the reality cast by the shadows of my own past.

As for my trials within death, which for me overtime have allowed for me to be raised up and made imperishable, as it was also for the namesake of my spirit As-Sala-Petra Selah, which had also evolved from out of the ruins of this Hellenistic destruction of the dead and death itself, which for me became my accomplished redemption, in that my life's prayer would be in little need of sustenance to nurture and support me with, as such was the abundance of the blossoms in their new seasoning and ripening, then as such was I upon my birth, except who for me who am I to turn too in yielding and becoming ready for such a harvest, for if the blossoms should remain unharvested, then perhaps they too shall once again become heavily laden and overgrown and fallen unto the ground and the spoils of the earth and wither and die, as too did I in waiting eagerly for my immortal glorification.

As it was during this period of time within Selah's forthcoming, that Angel Nephi had once again taken flight and ascended to the Empyreans, having brought this news to the attention of Haven, the newly appointed Herald Angel, having become deeply troubled that not all was as it had appeared to be concerning this his daughter Selah, as it was also upon this account that during his visit, in that somehow the entire household of the hosts of heaven, were already conscious of the forbidden rumors now being whispered and mentioned upon the lips of the Angels within this realm, in that an immortal had come into being, which if were found to be true, would cause many a rippling of unprecedented effects upon the whole of creation, in that the Angels of the Empyreans or at least Haven, would have to hold and summons the immortal unto the sanctions of this matter in their realm of the Kingdom, for no immortal of this description could be left permitted and allowed to live freely and unbound and unconstituted, to live and dwell upon the earth.

As I tell you Haven, albeit that my love beloved love and daughter is not of accordance with this world, but how can you be so certain Nephi that the grown child is as you say and suggest immortal, do you have any signs of proof of this, have you witnessed any miracles as said and set before you that might reveal it to be so, Nay Haven I have not, except that she exceeds far beyond any other basis of mortal intelligence, and so what is to be done with Selah I do not yet know, for if she is as I dare to say she is, well then I know that she must first come before the hosts of heaven, so that they might ascertain any such truth upon the assumptions regarding this matter.

Well yes Nephi you are right upon that account, but within my own wisdom I fear for her life and freedoms, for is Selah is as you declare immortal or not so, and we attempt to bring her here for to satisfy our own merits of curious conclusion, then will she not be affected by this ordeal and environment and surely die, well yes I see your referencing if she is not immortal then she will not survive amongst those of us within the empyreans, but on the other hand, if she is immortal as we may so understand to assume to believe, then there is no place at all between heaven and earth that will have any negative or damaging effects upon her whatsoever, and this is where the errors of indifference may give rise to our concerns, but to be sure of this predicament, then perhaps it is better that you and I should first descend and go to inquire after her for her own protection.

And so it was a conversation about a conversation that did indeed prompt with some urgency as to whom Selah could have been communicating with if not any of the Angels within the Empyreans, and so Haven the Herald Angel along with Nephi did descend to pay a visitation to Anahita and Selah, who was one that seemed to charmed and preoccupied with the simplicity of nature, and time, and the universe, as it was upon this intellect that Haven did seek to address her with.

Selah, love beloved love, do you know who I am, I do not, except that you are Haven are you not, yes I am, but do you know that I am a Herald, yes, then can I speak with you upon the importance of my presence now here in your company, yes you can Herald, well I wish to ask you a simple question of faith that would settle a puzzling question to rest if you may permit me too, what question of faith, well the question I propose to ask if you should seek to abide forth in answering me plainly and simply without it causing any displeasure of disdainment, my pleasures are none to feel disdainment about, but the question of plain and simple answers are noteworthy, in that you seek the truth and nothing but the truth, yes Selah, the truth that I seek to know, is if you are aware that you may be of an eternal or immortal embodiment, no, are you sure Selah, did you understand the proposed question, I ask you again are you immortal or not, no not yet, not yet, but what do you mean, you are either immortal or you are not, now which is it, it is the latter Herald I am not yet immortal, but is that to suggest that you will or shall become immortal, well yes, I see but how shall that come to arise and fulfill itself, it shall come, yes but how Selah how exactly.

Do not pressure her Haven, as she knows what she is, yes Anahita, but this is very important for multiple reasons, as I need to know what she knows, especially since I am Herald, as you know that I can help her to avoid any detentions and also help to aid her in every way shape and form, otherwise the Hosts of Heaven will be caused to move against her by the way of sanctioning her to give testimony, now Selah please explain, Explain what exactly, for the war of words, or the word wars that you have enlisted and unleashed of your own idle rhetoric of inferior meaning, which is a mark of insolence now found to be a deafening force drowning my ears with the sound of your infantile and internal unfounded assertions, if my examination is to be found fit enough to agree with your own misconstrued interpretations of what I am or am not to be Herald.

Nay Selah this is not the truth, it is only to deal with these matters accordingly, as I see that for some unknown reasons, you are vexed by my inquiry, well perhaps your inquiry is intrusive Haven, and so therefore in defiance and causing me such displeasure, I shall take to my accord, the silences of my own constitution, for what belongs to God returns to God, and what remains of Satan is detained by Satan, and so therefore what is of Selah, is also Selah's own, and so for whatever sanctions that you may attempt to hold me in contempt with, then you shall also consider what you have already withheld in my absence, but I don't understand Selah, what has been withheld from you.

It is that which is yet to be restored unto me to and put in its proper place along with the retrospective congruence and fullness of equality, Nay please Selah do not isolate and push us away, we are only seeking to support you, Nay Haven you must refrain from asking her any more questions, Anahita I only desire to help her, Nay Haven, if the truth cannot be proven or substantiated as a fact, and my daughter says, that she is yet to become immortal, then let her be, but that is my point Anahita, she is fully aware in acknowledging the truth of this reality at some point, yes but her life is her own life, and not yours to implement some meddlesome rule of judgment, and so if there is no answer, then she need not agree to do so.

Yes Anahita, but this will not change things if she chooses not to speak, well then at least allow me to intercede in mediating upon her behalf as her mother and advocate, now Selah if do not wish to speak in giving testimony of your faith to Haven, then just give me one nod to answer yes and two nods to answer no, do you understand, as she nodded only once her actions were made clear, then I must suggest Anahita, that Selah should accompany myself and Nephi to the Empyreans for her to be presented before the Hosts of Heaven, as they will also presume and seek to ask the same questions there that I am asking here, yes Haven, but I tell you, you will not get the definitive answer that you are seeking, and as she is not yet immortal, and if she does not survive the journey, then you are accountable for that as Herald, well that I cannot answer, but my instincts tells me, that this is exactly what she wants, wait, wait one moment before you go, as I must at least administer to my daughter, if you are to bring her to the other place.

My daughter and love beloved love of Nephi, I know that you have your reasons for pursuing this course of action, but even if you do not possess an answer for me as to why you must persist in this matter, the you must accompany your Father Nephi and Haven to accompany you and support you along the way, but in the essence of truth, we are all bound and answerable for our choices, I only hope that you will find the right answer for the right question at the right time to fulfill the future outcome that you are justified in seeking, as for now the moment of truth is upon and the test of time is upon you, and I pray and hope that you are prepared for this journey of ascension towards the spiritual body, for the only way to get to the truth is to come face to face with it.

And so it was that Anahita, had brought forth an elixir of a mixed dessicative powder and essences of ambrosia that she hoped would sustain and serve the intensity and enduring longevity, to help and aid Selah as she made transition from one place to the next, and so they took to flight beyond the firmament of the earthly stratosphere destined for the Empyreans, and as for Selah her spirit did not waver but began to flourish as they drew nearer and closer to destiny's calling, whilst steadily being held by her father Nephi and Haven the Herald Angel supporting her either side as they made their ascension.

As for Selah, her body did begin to suffer the universe's painful elements of time and space without the familiarity of the gravitational foundations of an earthly atmosphere to sustain it, and her breath and breathing were diminished, but she remained conscious throughout her will of determined fate, along with the excesses of speed they did arrive safely upon the threshold of the sanctuary and the abode of the Angels, that is the Empyreans, as it was upon this threshold that Haven's Angelic Father Simeon did appear to meet and to greet them, and as his eyes glanced upon Selah and her eyes did meet with his, that the memory of a bygone moment upon the passages of time crossed his mind, as if he too knew, that something telling had surpassed itself.

Father this is Selah, yes I already know who she is, but that being said, even now I can see that is not the same Selah from the days of yore, she is somewhat different since our first encounters within the reigns of Hark, but why does she not speak for herself, it is because my daughter has sworn an oath and vow of silences, well that may be so but when she is addressed by the Host's of Heaven and this assembly, she must speak and not withhold her tongue, or sanctions will be made against her, yes Simeon I promise you she will speak when spoken too, but I must relay to you that it may only of consequence as to which of the Angels amongst us has proven to know her innermost sanctum, well until those Angels have disclosed themselves before us, let us present ourselves to our host's upon high.

As none had seen or even witnessed the coming and the going forth of the Hosts of Heaven, except that they would appear and disappear and reappear within an indescribable form from time

to time, as they were somewhat premeditated in their approaches towards any other forces or energies that might be present, and so firstly although it is not a natural phenomenon to transgress or read the minds of Angels, although in truth it is through our obedient will that we do not think out of context or with contrary notions to be of another mind or will, as such if we are to pursue other intelligences that are not of our primordial nature, then we can easily become fallen Angels as our alliances may dictate, but we who are assured and steadfast, surely and truly know that there is only the divine will of heaven, and so although it may be simple to assume that actions or to know the will or mankind as we also know the instincts of animals and mammals within their own kingdom.

As it is only as Qonshushmign's, that we can penetrate beneath the veil to know the true nature of any and every soul, but that being said, the Hosts of Heaven come before these conscious minds, and are original within every aspect of the composition of the human heart and mind and soul and even spirit, but in all fairness, they are impartial and without conviction and judgment, as it is only the essence of truth within all realms of all kingdoms that is permitted the true freedom to go beyond in knowing no boundaries, a bit like the notes of the harp or the flute, or at least the tremor of instruments that travel freely upon the winds and the breeze and flow harmoniously in striking a chord of resonance throughout, and even breaching and revealing and yielding their sounds unto the cosmos of the universe, and so in coming forth, the Hosts of Heaven were first pronounced as, Monad the One, alongside Bythos the Aeon, alongside Proarkhe the Arkhe who within their characteristics and personalities, carry forth the greatest virtues of all, which are the forces transcendent of Thought, Grace, Silence, and Truth of Mind within the regions of light.

And so whether we have the ability or the choice to choose or to accept its merits' or not, as even they in their unwittingly and superior knowledge that they possess which even the Qonshushmign's would seek to dictate and to imposingly implement and place their sanctions and will upon the face of the world, then ask those who would call and recognize themselves as the dreamers of the Empyreans, who would wish and desire to express and to exercise their own judgments upon or over the face of the earth, as not being Man or Woman, but being quite simply Male and Female, the Hosts of Heaven proceeded in the presence of Selah in already knowing and possessing the several accounts of infinite outcomes and possibilities of all eventualities that would and were to arise, but in containing the processes of all warranted actions of determinations that still remained, as if history however repetitive was only happening because of the warrant and the cause of all perfections to become satisfied for the first time, as time in itself is timeless, and so with the reverberations of a thundering sound, and light of flashes, and the echoes of vibrations, surely it was felt, because it was known, and it was revealed, because it had already transpired that the Hosts of Heavens did communicate it rightly and simply and yet justly and profoundly so.

One of the sanctity's and promises of God to those of humanity who follow divine law, or whether the human being believes and accepts in the existence of the immaterial soul, also possesses the ability to be transformed, and to transform itself in achieving immortality is not at fault or a subject of myth or fantasy or speculation, except that it should not be found to be so easily achievable by any miraculous or ordinary feat, but requires complete and total dedication and devotion for this victory to be won, I Sayeth Monad the One.

But if these rights of passage are so seemingly endless within the succession of birth, life and then the destruction of death, in that they only detrimentally serve to obstruct and deny the immortal of humanity from going and coming forth with the rights to excel towards their own perfection aided only by the Angelic forces of those of us who determine it to be so, then let me ask you this, what is the purpose of their steps of ascension in faith, if we as the Hosts of Heaven, only serve to act to oppose it, especially when it is greatly achievable when necessary and needed as such an event of transcendence, or can it be an admission or default upon our own ethical reasoning being in this disposition in maintaining these Heavenly rankings, that upon this matter, however inextricably linked and woven into our fabric of creation, that we and humankind, however we choose to defy or acknowledge it, and in spite of these two harvests, that what we uphold and select for the governing harmony or all creation, has always maintained and brought with it the grace of God in its fullness, I Sayeth Bythos the Aeon.

And so what has become of this Angeldom, when we have not yet done away with such a contemptuous divisiveness, in that we still have managed to regress beyond our divine greatness, in that we have somehow managed to deny the rights of passage of an immortal of humankind any authority, or to be advantageous, and become risen and set upon high, in possessing or having any influence over our own elected positioning, well then it is notably so that upon reflection, that we have become not much unlike the fallen ones,

23

who through their own disloyal and insubordination thrown from up high and put asunder and wasted so lowly for this stance of viewpoint all along, I Sayeth Proarkhe the Arkhe.

Let it be known that although Selah holds her tongue through the grace of her own faith and convictions, that it would hereby serve to satisfy the Hosts of Heaven in its own agreeable nature, that this is not by no means a matter for consideration of condemnation or Hocuspocus within the translation of her Will, Hoc Est Enim Corpus Meum, which hereby defines the incantations or invocations of prayers notably intended for the salvation of God set upon on high, set against the destruction of death, Alakazam! In that it is the expression of the one trueness that has brought forth with it this present state of mind, body and soul, Abracadabra! Upon the threshold of this sanctuary that is Heavenly and Heavenbound, except that the translation of her Will is hereby as follows, I Sayeth Proarkhe the Arkhe.

And so it was with that statement of all intent and purposes, that Selah had ceased in her expressions of communication, and maintained her pious refrain and dignity of virtue with a motion of silence, which had caused the inquisitors of the Hosts of Heaven along with the Qonshushmign's to become confounded by the irony of their own curious examination of her, and so therefore causing the constraints of confusion to be borne, even amongst the highest ranking of the Angels of the Empyreans.

For she is not an Angel, and yet she has these angelic attributes, and yet she is silent, but resounds profoundly loudly, in her spirit which is eternal, but she is not yet immortal, and yet she is more than human, and yet she is destined but as of yet, to be meet with destiny, and so therefore much harder for her restoration to be realized, and so therefore she is incomplete, unless of course, the fulfillment of her prayer is found to be redeemed upon the pardonable declaration of the fullness of its own merits and satisfaction, I Sayeth Bythos the Aeon

As it is impartial for us, as well as impractical for us to impeach in saying one thing or two things, or even three things, then let it be known that Selah should be escorted and taken from this place, and should be delivered hereafter seeking to inquire to find the truth of her words within the Celestial Abode, as it may reveal to her the wherefore and the whereabouts of those that once revered as the chosen elite of Generals and Lieutenants, who went out before us amongst the playground the graveyards of this, the unknown and unchartered stars of Heaven, I Sayeth Monad the One.

Although no words were uttered or pronounced forth from Selah's lips within the conduct and presence of the Hosts of Heaven, it was not without fear or trembling upon her part, of that which her resolve was to be met, for if the Hosts of Heaven did not expose and reveal Selah's thoughts, then instead it would cause the rumors of her immortality to circulate unfounded throughout the Empyreans and also go unchallenged and unvetted without any real grounds, or proper root and foundation behind it, and by their doing so and foresight, this would quash and reveal itself to the awareness of this Angelic Household, whilst avoiding upsetting the equilibrium or disrupting and disuniting the cause of the Heavens to become unbalanced in her presence.

But as the sanctions had only proved itself to be partly sufficient within its value of instrumental gain, in that it would at least only decree the Hosts of Heaven to come to some conclusive aspects of suggestion as to what event should take place next concerning Selah, and yet as it was within the prolonging and pondering of their revisement, that soon enough, came forth out of the midst with the art of surprise and not a moment to lose or waste, and of course without any need of any formal introductions, did an Angel appear who was scarcely ever seen and yet recognizable to all throughout the Empyreans, and as he drew nearer and nearer, and closer and closer, he appeared to somewhat relieved and delightfully pleased to see the face of Selah standing the before the Hosts of Heaven, alongside her father Nephi, and also Haven the Herald Angel, who up until now, had also kept and maintained their position.

Greetings Monad the One, and Proarkhe the Arkhe, and Bythos the Aeon, but permit me if you will, but I would also like to suggest, that I would also like to accompany these fellow beings upon this flight of passage to the Celestial Abode, Ah yes to expect the unexpected, Pablo Establo Estebhan Augustus Diablo, and who else except none other than you, and we I see that you still possess the ability to make an unannounced and yet amazing entrance, so as to disrupt our deliberations, well isn't it nice to know that I never fail to give any validity or credence to any whispers of rumors that may echo throughout this place, but it would seem that this one were somewhat true wouldn't you agree my Hosts.

Now Pablo as you know very well and are truly aware, that this is not a place of which to make light humor and idle mockery in our presence and proceedings, so do not perform all manner of wit, and cause all mannerisms of jovial trifling, nay pray tell and please forgive Pablo my Hosts for my tedious sentiments of expression oh wise ones, but after but after all, is this not a joyous occasion, but allow me to quicken the moment for now, for if you allow me to do your bidding, I bid you adieu, in that we might hasten our beloved Selah to the Celestial Heavens, as I am certain patiently awaits her beckoning and calling, as it would bring great pleasure for us to meet with and to entertainment our celestial sisters, very well then Pablo, it is granted that you too shall accompany them, so let it be done according to that merit, I Sayeth Monad the One.

And so it was that Selah and her Angelic father Nephi, along with Haven the Herald Angel, and now with the recent arrival of Pablo Establo Estebhan Augustus Diablo, the Immortal One, would journey on beyond, from one abode to the next, as they would for now have to extend themselves to support Selah beyond this present horizon, in order to travel effortlessly unto this Celestial expanse awaiting, but this time it was not to be one of ordeal orchestrated and choreographed to maintain and befit a perfect projected outcome, for this time the influence of Selah upon the heavens of the earth, had by now permeated and penetrated like wild flowers bursting forth from within the depths of the ground trodden beneath, as she was by now made ready and prepared for the past and the present to lay the way straight towards the future of which she was eagerly in anticipation of and waiting for.

Pray tell us Nephi, but when was the it last that Selah spoke, and also pray tell us, what promises does she seek to release and undo her tongue, well I can tell you Pablo, that she first withdrew from speaking when I first invited Haven to communicate with her, except that it wounded and vexed her, of why I do not know, but as to when she might permit herself to speak also I do not know except that this time had not yet come forth or arisen unless, unless what Nephi, unless she is to address the one who is the rock of her foundations, well perhaps the Celestial Angels can assist and help to enlighten Pablo as to what are the missing pieces of this puzzle in revealing the greatest hidden treasures that remain unsolved beneath this jigsaw, and where they may be buried and uncovered to give voice and sound to this virtue of silences.

As it was upon this unrehearsed threshold, that they did all arrive upon the abode of the celestial Angels, who instantly appeared before them although somewhat surprised to see Pablo the Immortal alongside Haven the Herald Angel, both of whom they had met once before, but that it was for the first time that Selah and her father who had heard of the Angels of Celestial Heavens, of whom they did not know and yet upon Selah's presence, they were instantly attracted to her natural and yet ordinary peaceful and pleasant spirit, in being so warm, that they took her to the bosom of their hearts.

Greetings we welcome you Empyreans, but who amongst you is this one, she is my daughter Selah, and who are you I am Nephi of the Nephilim, yes Nephi of the Nephilim, but what is she, oh I see, well my daughter is increasingly and moreso of an immortal transition, then she is becoming like God is she not, Nay Celestials, allow me to explain, I have seen the places of where God resides, and she has not, and so therefore she in not God, Stand down Herald, but why should I Pablo, because no Angel of the Empyreans has seen or witnessed God, nay Pablo it is true, he has seen it, but even if I the Immortal One have not seen it, then why Haven, well I believe that the Heralds are just that little bit appropriately properly placed to see such pinnacles.

So she is becoming God, nay she is not, she is fulfilling the promises of a prayer I tell you, but tell us for what does she pray for if she is becoming God, nay she is not yet immortal my celestial ones, except that she is becoming as you say, so she must only pray for the love of her beloved love to obtain a miracle perhaps, or a blessing as an earth mother, tell us Earth Mother, who is this beloved love, her beloved love is the Herald, but which Herald, speak Haven, the Herald is Hark but I am Herald now, Stand down Haven, this is important to know for us all to be concerned with, as the question remains, where is Hark now, I told you he resides with God, I have seen it upon the rotation of the wheels of the Ophanim, upon the Ophanim, you say, yes, so too did Selah's first Angelic Son Stefan see it also, you can ask to inquire of the Angel of Mercy and the Angel of Justice, if you do not accept the reasoning and the revelation of my account, then we must gather ourselves amongst these celestials to learn more about God.

Pray tell us what you thought you had seen Haven, I did all but see the face of God, but I saw for the first time the Archangels, and they stood tall over the place that separates and partitions God from us, and us from God, a partition you say, guarded by the Archangels, Uriel, Raphael, Michael, Raguel, Zerachiel, Gabriel and Remiel, no wonder I could not go forth in my wandering and seeking to no avail to find and discover it in that I could not permeate beneath such a simple measure as a partition fortified by the Archangels, yes that's it exactly, what I had seen, except the Angel of Mercy and the Angel of Justice would have seen if for they had not fled from the sights, Yes! yes, I mean nay for Selah is not without God, but she is not

God, but she is destined if only of God's love and graciousness, were upon her, the she will enter the kings kingdom of the heavens of the heavenly universe, now come and go forth Celestials, and summons in and bringing Mercy and Justice to witness our presence here, for they shall fulfill the prophecy of the immortality of humankind.

Mighten I also speak in professing to say, that there in another, another who, there is another one of a celestial embodiment, that granted us the courage to go beyond the furtherest reaches of transcendence other than what we had experienced or known before, but what is this, who knows where we can breach past the unbreachable depth, I do not know except that she knew us, a Celeste you say, nay her name is liken to the Aura, an Aura, but which angel possess such an enchanting name, that it is so simple and yet less obvious to us of determination, are we not all destined for the simplest of virtues in life, how are we to find this Aura who possess this bestowment upon creation, I am certain that she will come, yes but how did she come to know you before, I do not know except that it was for or preparedness to come present before the Ophanim and the throne of God.

And what became of your bestowment Haven, I still possess it within me and upon the depth and breadth of my wings, I can go wherever it wills me to go, but how are we to pass if we do not possess such blessings also for our ascensions on high, I do not know Pablo, but perhaps I can find her or at least try to summons her here to address us if it is God's will, yet but everything is God's Will and not our own effective doing, go and find her, and bring her to attend to our matters outstanding, as we shall abide until your return, I will attend to the Angelic Celestial Embodiment of the Angelic Aura, in finding and knowing who having bestowed upon us, the ability to act in accordance and to be at one with the Cosmos and Universe, having decorated us with a blessing sent forth from the most divine and ubiquitous virtue within creation, now how am I to find such a virtuous one, who grants blessings with Halo's set upon the forehead like a crown.

And upon that moment of clarification that Haven had alighted and departed company, that the Angel of Mercy and the Angel of Justice did appear before them, except that they did not know that they would be called to give an allied response to Haven's recollection and sincere recording of the whereabouts of God's Heavenly Abode and dwelling place, partitioned away somewhere within or upon the whole of creation, except that they could not concur as Haven had said, that they had fled prematurely before it was revealed to them, and so upon this outcome that the last thing they had witnessed was the disappearance of Ophlyn the Herald Angel, but it would be by this account and admission and realization that Selah would begin to become enlightened in knowing and in realizing that all who mattered to her ascension were now present and in prime position to achieve the unachievable and impossible feat, of unlocking the mysteries concerning the love of the beloved love, and so it was there and then that Selah spoke the words.

Invictus and in victory, I shall embrace my immortality, tell me Justice what were the last words of Ophlyn before he ceased to be, his words Selah were somewhat vague upon my recollection, but I believe that he said Ab Origine, and he spoke it out of defiance and weakness and with great sorrow, yes I would imagine that he would, and why is that Selah, well it is simply because he must have known it could also bring him back, back, back from where, why from the very beginning, of what my celestial sister, of himself, as it is an oath of consecration, in being that we must die to live, and sometimes live to die, yes I see, but I did not think it could be a summons of any sort, nay you did not because you fled, but as an earth mother I too am also permitted to hold these virtues of expression of incantations, and invocations, as we have already said between ourselves that the love of the beloved love is oh so powerful, that only a true servant such as I could die to live for it, and now live to die for it.

Now listen and pay heed and attention perfectly and attentatively, and with open hearts and open minds, that when Haven returns with the Celestial Angelic Aura, I request that Pablo shall do my bidding at once and go forth out into the world and seek out, Kali Ma, and Josephine Stiles, and carry out and deliver a message, that I Sayeth As Sala Petra Selah, in revealing to them, with accurate accordance the verity of sanction, the last words of these Herald Angels, and also my that of my beloved Stefan, as I am now sure that this is the passage of rites, that will take us beyond the partitions that separate us from God and God from us.

Even in the void there are an infinite group of stars as having being unchartered, and as it is, some are dying, and as it is some are just beginning to be born, for these are the stars that are the dreams of the Angel Babies, and so what are the recesses and the progressive patterns and structures of such indivisible and innumerable compositions, for if a star is indeed dying within the cosmos and the fabric of the universe, then what are the traces and remnants left behind in the vast wide open expanse that encompasses all, for out of the void I did hear the sounds of expressions resounding throughout like a voice calling out to me,

Haven Come Up Here**, but I did not see from where the light in this universe would guide me up there, as from nowhere it came.**

Where are you I said upon reply, I am here Haven, all aglow, but where in the illuminations of life are you to be seen, it is here within the void of these living and dying embers, do you desire for me to explode with might and magnitude, or do you expect me to quietly and gently fade away, please Aura do not amuse yourself with me and keep me in state of limbo, reveal yourself, but what shortened patience that you possess Haven, are you not looking for me, yes I am Aura, for it is an urgent matter that you I wish for you to materialize before me, why are you afraid of the dark matter of the universe, nay Aura it is not the dark matter that I fear, I only fear God, very well then, I shall come down and share my presence with you once again.

And instantly the Aura did appear before Haven, are you friend or foe, please Aura do not tally with, for I am your friend for true, yes but don't you think that time changes everyone and everything around us upon its journeying, don't you agree, well yes I do agree, but time has not changed in me, oh but it has Herald, for when we first met upon our original engagement you were not crowned as you are now, yes I do see it now, please forgive me as you are correct in your observations of me, then what does it suit you to now be the Herald Angel of all the Empyreans, it is an honor my Aura and my also my duty and task to fulfill such a position of great importance, then why have you come to see me out in the place, are you not blessed enough with all kinds of amazements, well yes Aura, I am humbled by such blessings and accorded responsibility, but please hear me out before you choose to expel or turn me away from this place, I will not do such a thing to you Herald, as I have seen that you hold honor and virtue in your response, but pray tell me, the Empyreans, do they sing and favor you with voice and songs, yes Aura, they do, then that is enough to keep you company and safely defended from falling from grace.

Now pray tell me what is it that you wish for me to do for you, well my Aura it is to accompany myself to the celestial abode, and for what heavenly reason Haven, well it is to bestow a gift of the Halo upon my earthly and sentient companions, but why do they require such an act to be performed upon them, well it is because of the beatification of a human soul, born of Angelic beings, a human soul, yes, a human being the heavens have made her immortal if she is not so already, but I have not been granted or commanded to do so Herald, but please hear me Aura, as only you possess the keys to such a destiny of promise, are you not aligned as being on the right side of God, yes perhaps I am, but your request, it disturbs me, now Haven, allow me to be alone once more until such an appointed time that our alliance should require it.

And so it was that Haven having been turned around by the request and instruction of the Celestial Angelic Aura, that for some peculiar feeling he had become somewhat disheartened, in that he would have to make his way back to celestial abode with some news of disappointment, in that he would have to inform Pablo the Immortal One, that the Aura would not be in attendance in fulfilling the prophecy of their cause concerning the duly awaiting beatification of Selah, but as to whether it was before, or during, or after their meeting that something would once again begin to influence all that were somehow intrinsically connected to the immortality of Selah's prayers, and of what she was to become.

You have returned to us Haven, but you are alone, so pray tell us where is the Celestial Aura and what news do you bring us, the news I bring Pablo is one I'm afraid to say, and that is that the Aura is not so willing and forthcoming to aid us and bless us with her presence, but why, why has she refused our request, is she not aware of the importance of this matter pertaining to be, I cannot speak for the Aura Pablo, except that I cannot know the true answer, as you can see that it has also come upon me as a feeling of dreaded awareness that not all is within our control to know its eventual outcome, even I as Herald now realize that I cannot support and sustain every account of action, and accord with it precisely.

Nay Haven do not falter and dismiss all as lost, for you have done what was expected and required of you, but pray tell me one thing, and what may that be Selah, tell us what were Hark's last words before entering the heavens of the heavenly universe, well Selah, as I feared the worst for my own deliverance, I do recall, before being seated upon the Ophanim, that his last words having being uttered were, Ab Aeterno, spoken and witnessed by myself and the Archangels, even though it may have been somewhat spoken reluctantly as he entered therein, Ab Aeterno, yes Selah, those are the words of wisdom that I now confess and relay to you, yes Ab Aeterno, these are the words that I need to hear, and the words that I cannot bare to live without.

Now the preponderance of them and of those in bearing the gift of the Aura, that is embedded beneath their outwardly appearance is simply because of this, in that God would know them as they are and not as what they would attempt to conceal or to present and display themselves as so to be, although any Angel bearing the gift of the Aura, it was only to expose the true

34

identity and sincere nature of all souls in their spiritual form, as any soul affirmed with the Halo, was proven to be of a particular nature of being that which God knows, and what is and what is not revealed to creation within its' perfection in having no falsity or falsehood about it.

But the very idea that a human being of Selah's description, as being said to have afforded in being worthy of such rites and rituals of beatification, is one act that may only be ordained and proven by God and his Angels, and so for this Aura to be uninstructed in addressing this particular matter, would have to consider the weight and the gain of this matter independently, if she were to choose to go forth and grant such a blessing, if the news that Haven had relayed to her were found to proven and to be true, as the Aura knew, that in being true to herself, that God would of had to commanded it to be so, and so in order for it to become fulfilled in its ambitions, then such was the pondering of what is of God and what is not, as it is also the same to ask what is the divine will of purpose.

For Haven as Herald had requested it, but not of himself but of another, of humankind, who are by all standards, seen as a being of a different accord, as one is wholly obedient while the other has the free will of mind and spirit to choose otherwise, and yet all are overwhelming in God's grace and love, and so the Celestial Angelic Aura, had considered this matter much before making her descent from the void, as she journeyed toward the abode of the Celestial Angels.

Selah it would appear that this one has responded to our request, as I see that it is the celestial Aura that we witness descending before us, yes it is Selah, except that I thought she would not come, nay Haven but she has, for it seems that this one has heard you in the bargaining of your plea to aid us, or perhaps she has thoughtfully known all along that this is the way of heaven, so how could she not attend to us upon her own reflections and duty, are we not all God's Creation eventually destined to be found Heavenbound, now, let us see what is to said in our preparedness as come before the Aura.

Who amongst you is the deified chosen one, for none other shall answer until it is revealed to me, I am the one of whom you should seek to address Aura, and what is the purpose of your faithful claim that I am permitted to stand here before you, my faith my celestial aura, is only to kindle the love and beloved love of my beliefs in that which is my exalted rock of salvation, but what love is this found amongst you and these faithful of all eternity, my love, it is only to be found within sanctuaries of heaven and my Herald, then so it shall be, that you the Earth Mother Selah, shall be given over to the love and the exhalations of a Herald now pronounced and proclaimed in the Heavens of the Heavenly Universe, and who else amongst you shall be deemed fit and willing and worthy to accompany Selah upon this transcendental journey.

My Aura, upon my trial and examination of this journey, I only desire and wish to appeal to you with my heart and mind, that the Halo upon that with which you lift up life unto Him, that you shall also allow those of whom are of my restoration, shall also be found to be fit and willing and willing in such receivership to be granted and made worthy with a blessing, if the so wish, then from here on and henceforth, the Celestial Angelic Angel of the Aura shall also bestow upon them that are found to be fit and willing to follow hereafter Selah, into this dwelling place.

And so it was that Celestial Angelic Aura, did bestow the profound blessings of the Halo, and set to place it as a crown firstly and firmly upon the head of Pablo the Immortal One, followed by Nephi and then lastly upon the head of Selah, in that before she and her fellow sentient beings would now be prepared and ready to begin their ascension, and so it was that Selah had instructed Pablo to go and seek out Josephine Stiles, the beloved love of Stefan, and to reveal to her, the last spoken incantation of Stefan, Ab Incunabulis, and then also to seek out Kali Ma, and also reveal to her the last spoken incantation of Ophlyn, Ab Origine, so that they too could come forth from out of the world, in knowing that the Aura had ordained it concerning the fate of the Heaven of the Heavenly Universe.

A gift comes in many forms, and even sometimes disguised as miracles, which are often less than frequent to take effect and transpire between us, as otherwise they would not be miracles if they occurred all the time, and so it was that upon their ascension and flight towards the fulfillment and dwelling place of such promises, that Pablo the Immortal One, did indeed take to flight and part company set for a new adventure, as he departed from Haven the Herald Angel, and Nephi the Nephite of the Nephilim, and Selah, and that of the Celestial Angelic Angel of the Aura, and the Angel of Justice, and the Angel of Mercy to go in search of Josephine Stiles and Kali Ma, if only to deliver a divine message of great importance, in that they would also come to know and learn the answers of the question of their own love and beloved love, that up till now would have kept them in the dark, as if it were that time itself had come to give up and reveal its secrets, in that all it had once taken away from that which was by now to be brought back together.

The last if not the least of the Earth Mothers, Josephine Stiles, was by now at this stage living a faithful and spiritual and holistic lifestyle, although somewhat of a independent and solitary soul, her world was not the same without Stefan to share it, as it was some time ago when the Aura had first come to bestow the blessings of the Halo upon him, that Josephine had somehow known and also come to accept all along as an Earth Mother, that this was the way of all things pertaining to the roles and abiding duties and responsibilities of Angel, and so it was that with all things, that when Pablo the Immortal One, had first come to appear before her, that somehow through the hopes of Heaven, that a miracle could now somehow be revealed.

Pray tell me Earth Mother, but am I to believe that you are the one named Josephine Stiles are you not, yes, yes I am the one, but who mighten you be my Angel, my name as I declare it, is Pablo Establo Estebhan Augustus Diablo, the Immortal One, and I am humbled to present myself before you, but I come bearing a message of the one you may recall as being Selah, Pablo you say, yes Mother I am he, well I have heard of you before, and it is not true to say that you are the one who wanders the heavens to and fro from the six depths to the seventh highs, well yes that is also true to say that I wander by the above and the beneath of one way to the next, then tell me what is the message that you are instructed to reveal to me, well Mother, because of the life and also because of the destruction of death itself, I pray that you will heed to take note and comprehend that time has made all things considered, but before I tell and inform you of the nature of my visit, I need for you to think and consider, that as an Earth Mother, and in all that you have done in your beliefs of philanthropy and altruism, and compassion and empathy, as even when your faith in the here and now, and also in looking back through the memories of melancholy, thinking about today and everyday and even the future, for the message that bear and now convey to you, shall also gather you up and swallow you up along with all of your feelings and emotions and promises of encouraging expressions of the love of your beloved love, Angel Stefan.

As it was instantly upon hearing the name of her beloved Stefan remarked upon and from the lips of Pablo, that Josephine in shock and surprise, fell to her knees, as if weakened and broken by the emotional pains of loss and regret and a labor of loneliness's and sorrows gone by, and justly so, Pablo assisted in lifting Josephine to her feet in witnessing her tears of despair, a woman who has struggled infinitely with great trials and burdens in the absence of her beloved.

What is the message that you bear gatekeeper, the message that I bear, are also the profound words in incantations that that you are too mediate and pray upon, is as told to you, Ab Incunabulis, **and with that Pablo the Immortal One, did not stay to remain, but before leaving, he did inform Josephine, that she would be visited by the Celestial Angelic Angel of the Aura, as he departed knowing that this message upon its translation, would be the beginning and the start of the miracle and its transformation of Josephine Stiles.**

As it were so, that as Pablo the Immortal One, sought to seek out and locate Kali Ma, that Selah who was by now in flight and being supported by her Angelic Father Nephi, along with Haven the Herald Angel and the Angel of Justice and the Angel Of Mercy, and the Celestial Angelic Angel of the Aura, as with each and every element and rippling strand of life arising out of

the dark matter, that they journeyed through the cosmos, guided only by the infinite relativity of time, for they were the sentient beings having sustained in coming towards the end of chaos, and pandemonium, and turmoil, and upheaval, and disruption, as they were by now entering into the presence of a pure and yet primal environment, guided only by the Halo with which they all possessed.

As they had by now journeyed through the infinite void of dark matter, where they happened to come upon the edge of a black hole that had once delivered up Ophlyn the Herald Angel, and Angel Stefan, and Hark the Herald Angel from this place to the next, and yet it was upon this eventful horizon, that Nephi had considered if he should endure to remain to go forward without his love and beloved love Anahita, Selah's mother besides him.

Pray tell me what is this place Aura, this my fellow sentient beings, is the point of no return, as from the birth of a star, and the dreams of the angel babies, which have given way to the multitude of spiritual descendants that became souls, souls of which we inhabited, as for the fertile atmospheric waters that gave way when we fell from the heavens, where we were once also a part of the whole of creation, as with each precious measure, that once we were separated as single droplets in the creation of single soul, that one by one, we as individual streams of consciousness, went out into the four corners, in that upon our fulfillment of prophecies that each soul would return.

Consider me for this purpose Aura, but I must abstain and refrain from this journey as I am deterred by some reservations and doubt without Anahita my love beloved love besides me, nay Nephi do not fret or fear for the future becoming, for the entire household of Selah shall be granted the freedoms of this passageway, but how can that be my Aura, surely it shall be, that when you come face to face with the Archangels, that they in turn will address you in kind, and promise, and with all comprehension, for all things did already begin to return to their original composition, as even I the Celestial Angelic Anger of the Aura, am also required to place the remoteness of all Halo's upon the brow and the forehead of that being which is Anahita and mother of Selah.

And so it was that they entered thereof beyond the event horizon albeit with the exception of the Celestial Angelic Angel that bears the Halo of Aura's, as she watched and looked on, as one by one, Nephi, and Haven, and the Angel of Justice, and the Angel of Mercy along with Selah, did enter in the black hole and were to be seen and gazed upon no more by the Aura.

Upon finding Kali Ma, and upon her receiving the truth as told by Pablo the Immortal One of this revelation, Kali Ma was somewhat elatedly happy and relieved to learn that Selah had come into her own fulfillment and fruition, even as Kali was very ecstatic in her rejoicement, and so without concealing the joy that overcame her, she was by now already preparing herself for what promises were awaiting to be received upon this bestowment from the Celestial Angelic Angel of the Aura, and So Kali Ma began to focus upon her prayers and meditation along with the reflection of Ophlyn's last words, Ab Origine, as revealed to her, somewhat causing her to feel an overwhelming and tremendous feeling of assurance, that perhaps, and surely enough, she would once again see the love of the beloved love again.

And so it was to be that after the revelations of the messages had become delivered, then so too was Pablo the Immortal One, now set and destined to make his ascension and way through to the infinite void of dark matter to seek out his fellow sentient beings, and to find the greatest expectations that now lay before him, and so without reservation, the Aura who was still also present and in prepared readiness to do her own bidding, did see Pablo for the last time as she readily alighted and departed company from this place in order to perform the final aspects of this rites of passage for those of whom had received the gifted messages of deliverance Anahita, Kali Ma, and last but not least Josephine Stiles.

It is time, yes Pablo it is, then I must bid you farewell Aura, for the yearning gates of the heavens now await me beyond this point and place in time of no return, yes, it does Pablo, now you must go and see that you join the others who have already succeeded you upon this transcendental happening and occurrence, as I must also now leave you to attend to these matters that are outstanding.

And so it was that Pablo the Immortal One, did enter into the black hole, and go beyond into the portal of this eventful horizon, as much to his amazement and discovery, he was soon to come across Selah, and Nephi, and Haven, and the Angel of Justice, and the Angel of Mercy who were all there to meet and greet him upon his succession in becoming, as such was the veil that had become lifted and uncovered by their eyes, in witnessing all that was there where they stood in the presence of the Ophanim and the Archangels, who were somewhat vigilant and in a posturing of readiness, and yet fixed and motionless, as if they had expected something of a great and profound degree to occur or

unfold at any given moment upon the reception of these sentient beings.

As the place in which the Archangels stood, was not one of majestic display, or awesome bewildering amazement, nor was it something so astonishly beyond fantastic, or to be described as wondrous or beautiful, but it was still somewhat profoundly striking within its remoteness, in being a place possessing an air of mysterious presence, fueling energy and vibrancy, pulsating and infusing the elements of the stars that filled the cosmos, with euphoric like auroric gaseous lights of green and blue, and purple and turquoise, that lit up and illuminated thereabouts embedded within the universe.

As it was to the left of the Ophanim, that the Archangels stood, which was somewhat magnified in its' solitary standing of where the Archangels maintained their forthright stance and position, almost overlooking it, and guarding the partition from their point of observation, which would only seem to serve and to suggest that a Godly like nature of creation were somehow apparent in spirit, and infinitely existing, laying beyond this dwelling point.

As it was unfathomable and unbeknown to them at first, except that the Aura had said, that all things were being transformed, in that they were only in a temporary state as transient beings, but in being in possession of the Halo, that they would now find that they could become reformed and reshaped in the midst of this place, and that this blessing of the Aura, inside and beneath the physical attributes of their natural being of this phenomenon, would begin to dematerialize, leaving only that which was uniquely consistent with the matter and the substance of the Aura's Halo, whilst both preparing and allowing them to be loosened from their current form, shedding the constraints whilst nurturing and sustaining the senses with the freedoms of the non physical form and constructed environment, in that they were all becoming the constellations that were all around and about them.

For a moment in time, they all became aware of this new and uplifting transformation, as there is the midst of where the Ophanim were placed, it still appeared to be actively interchanging by the multitude of innumerable souls within a millisecond of one another, as if time were somehow relentlessly affecting and yet unaffected by the speed and precision of predestination and predetermined outcomes of each and every aspectual consistency of all probability and eventuality, but then for some reason of redefining this current event, the Ophanim had now begun to slow down and to halt its' progressive cycle of interactive functioning, and then it ceased and stopped completely to turn or to rotate, until it remained empty and devoid of any and all things.

As for Haven the Herald Angel in recognizing that he would have to assume the affirmative, in that he would have to initially assert his position and break with the silences first, in being of the presence of this exceptional and uniquely indifferent protocol as comparable to the Empyreans, but before he even uttered a word, then so was it that Selah did speak the words of Ab Aeterno, and for some unknowing reason the Archangels broke rank and file, and stood aside from the place in which they appeared to be guarding and defending and protecting, and

then without notice or expectation, Hark the Herald Angel did appear to come forth in emerging from out of the partition, with both majestic greatness and yet graciousness in his presence, and he did begin to show and display and his acknowledgment to the Archangels before, whom also acknowledge him, before he humbly addressed his fellow Angels and sentient beings and that of course Selah.

Ab Aeterno from the infinitely remote, and from the very beginning, we are all considered by the creator to be eternal, as we are all created as much as we are uncreated, we are still of creation, in that with each and every infinite detail, and with each and every trial and perhaps adventure, along with each and every stride of momentum, and with every heartbeat and every teardrop, as with each and every element of touching space and time, and even without a single whisper or pronouncement of a word, we are God, and God is us, not just One, but the whole of creation, for the wheels have stopped for now, and will only resume to turn once again, after seven thousand, and six hundred and sixty five earthly days, as should quantify the necessary time, in both giving and allowing the time for the entire household of Selah to make their transition from that world to their heavenly ascension of this one, my love, beloved love As Sala Petra Selah.

Authors Notes

It is of the utmost importance that we do not destroy any persons personal faith, no matter what or how profoundly they may aspire to be inspired to believe in something quite supernaturally or unfathomable, so please consider this and find it in your heart to know that faith is in the expression of living a life of piety and filled with a magnitude of love, as some of us put our faith in people as much as each other, as much as people put their faith in God or Angels or Spirits or Science, so I only say this, that with faith, it is only an attempt and a positive attitude that we are affirmed and just, in believing that the narratives that we are all aiming to pursue and fulfill and uncover, is to be accordingly just and right and true in our pursuits in this life, as such is the faith, that I have in all of you.

The Angel Babies Story for me, was very much written and inspired by many feelings of expression, that was buried very deeply inside of me, as it was through my own exchanges, and relationships, and journeying, and upon the discovery of both negative and positive experiences, that often challenged my own beliefs, and personal expectations of what I thought or felt was my own life's purpose, and reason for being and doing, and very much what any one of us would expect to be the result, or the outcome of their own personal life choices based upon the status quo of our own design or choosing.

The story within itself, very much maintains its own conception of intercession from one person to another, as we can only contain the comprehension of the things that we most relate too, and that which most commonly resembles and reflect our own emotions and experiences, by tying in with something tangible that either connects, or resonate at will deeply within us, as many of us have the ability and intuit nature, to grasp things not merely as they are presented to us, but how things can also unfold and manifest in us, that are sometimes far beyond our everyday imaginings, and that are also equally hard to grasp and somewhat difficult to comprehend and let alone explain.

As we often learn to see such challenges and difficulties as these, especially in young minds, that react in responsive ways and are also equally gifted, or equally find it in themselves in life changing circumstances, to deal with prevailing situations, that most of us would take for granted, and would naturally see as the average norm, as we are all somewhat uniquely adjusted to deal with the same prevailing situation very differently, or even more so to uniquely perceive it in very different ways.

As for the question of how we all independently learn to communicate through these various means of creative, or artistic, or spiritual measures, is also simply a way of communicating to God as in prayer, as well as with one another, as all aspects are one of the same creation, as to whether such forms of expression can personify, or act as an intermediate medium, or channel to God, or indeed from one person to another, is again very much dependent upon the nature of its composition and expression, and the root from which it extends, and so for us to believe that our forbearers, or indeed our ancestors have the ability to intercede for us in such spiritual terms upon this our journey through life, is very much to say, that it is through their life's experiences, that we have become equipped, and given a wealth, and a portion of their life's history, with which for us to make our own individual efforts and choices, for us to be sure and certain of the way, in which we shall eventually come to be.

When we take a leap of faith, it is often into the unknown, and it is often associated with, or stems from the result of our constant fate being applied and presented to us in the context of a fear or phobia, insomuch so, that we must somehow, or at least come face to face with, or deal with, or come to terms with these matters arising, that are usually our own personal concerns, or worries, or anxieties toward a balanced or foreseeable reality, which is often beyond our immediate control, in that we are attempting to define and deal with this systematic physical, and spiritual progression, in the hope and the faith that we can resolve these personal matters, so as to allow us to put the mind and the heart at ease and to rest.

As it is often through our rationalizing, and our affirmation, and our professing or living with our beliefs, that what we often call, or come to terms with through our acceptance, is that through faith, belief and worship in God, that such personal matters, can easily be addressed, and dealt with, so as to overcome when facing such difficult and challenging obstacles, as even when in response to a negative impact that can have a harmful effect upon our physical bodies and being, we also often rely upon this same faith in the physical terms of our living and well being to guide us, and especially where we are often engaged in rationalizing with this phenomena, in the context of our faith, hope and belief, which often requires and demands us to look upon the world in a completely different way, so that we can reach far beyond the rational expectations of our own reality, and perceive to look forward into that of our metaphysical world.

As it is through this metaphysical world of all irrationality, and chaos and confusion, that a leap of faith is required to pass through and beyond the unknown context of our rational and conscious reality, and thus so as far as we can see, to understand our consciousness, as we believe it should be, in that we are contained in every aspect of our faith, hope and belief, as we are often presented with more than just a rational imagination, of what lies beyond our eventful fate or worries and concerns, and so within the mind of dreams, we are presented with a super imagination, where extraordinary things exist and take effect much beyond our physical comprehension, although very much aligned to the interconnectedness within our emotions, that brings with it a super reality, where we can accept the tangibility of these dreams upon realizing them, so as to be found and understood, as when we are found to be waking up in our day to day reality and activity, but also in choosing not to deny or extinguish these dreams as mere dreams, but to accept, and to see them, or refer to them as signs.

As of when we see such tell tale signs, or such premonitions forgoing, or foreboding us in our fate, it is very much that these signs often impact the most upon that of our conscious minds, as they are very much presented to us in an informative and abstract way, very much like a picture puzzle that we are busily attempting to piece together and work out, and very much in the way that we are attempting to put the heart and the mind at ease and to rest, so as to secure peace of mind in order to find and establish and maintain inner peace, as such signs as these, are often the ones that I am referring too, and can often and easily be presented to us in many ways, but to be sure and certain, if they are Godly or Divining messages upon intuition and translation, very much depends and largely relies upon us as individuals, as to what we are naturally engaged in and pursuing, in the same hope and light of the context, of this experience of such a Godly nature.

As such experiences are crucial and key, as to how we deal with any or all relationships, especially when we are developing a relationship within the Godly aspects of our lives, as more often than not, when we use such phrases and metaphors as, 'Going through a Door' or 'Crossing a Bridge, it is simply by saying such statements as these, or putting things in this way or context, that we decidedly know and acknowledge that a big change is about to occur, and develop or happen to us, and so we in ourselves are becoming equipped and prepared to deal with such changes, as they shall determine what shall be the eventual outcome of our fate, as there may already have been so many foretelling signs, much before the final impact or infinite sign is presented to us, insomuch so, that it may have already been subtly presented to us, much before the true perspective or picture of our reality has come to fruition and presented to us as a whole.

The whole being, is that which pieces itself together, with all the necessary facets and aspects of our Human Nature, Personality, Mannerisms and Characteristics and Traits, as all in all, it presents to us a vision, which sets us apart from one another, but also equally ties us all together in the event and act of completing our picture and journey through life, and it is through these instincts that we all naturally possess, and is all that is inextricably woven into the metaphysical fabric and the spiritual aspects of the heart and mind, and of those that are channeled along the lines of the minds meridians, and the intricate channels that give way to apprehensible intuitive mental awareness of signs and dreams, and or premonitions or visions, of how, or what we may choose to accept, or to objectively analyze, or to take note of and perceive in communication, or indeed how God may choose to communicate with or through us.

As it is in our realizing that within our personal fate and decisiveness, that we are calling upon, and facing a reality, that questions and presents itself to us all, as something that is profoundly spiritual and ambiguous, in relation to what we are all intrinsically held and bound by within our faith and beliefs, in that what we expect is about to unravel itself before us, as we begin to discover all that in which we are, as such is the expectation and the realization in our phobias and fears, that we may begin to readdress or even regress, or desist in such a course of action concerning these doubts and deliberations, so as not to offset or to promote any ideas that may bring about any personal demise, or disharmony, or disunity, that may trigger any negative aspectual forecasts or emotions within ourselves, as it is such a self fulfilling reality, that we are all in subjection too, in creating along and upon our own individual paths of merits and natural progression, that naturally such phenomena is presented and revealed to us as a whole, and is often profoundly real and yet maintains its simplicity, and is quite ordinarily so upon our realization of it, as if by mere chance that somehow deep down we already knew, that when we became aware of it, we somehow knew it to be so.

As it is these lessons in life, that are to be learnt from such self affirming challenges, so as to test our minds imagination and of course that which is at the very heart, of how we in our Human nature, can so easily push our abilities far beyond the boundaries, upon the premise of what is, or what is not possible, which brings to mind the verse and saying of the scripture and that is to say, that if anyone adds or takes away from this book, then so too shall their part be added or taken away, and yet if we continue further along this point, it also goes on to ask, who is worthy to remove this seal, so as to reveal the dream or the foreknowledge that we may all come to terms with our natural agreement and acceptance of it, as it is in knowing and accepting what shall befall us in our fate, as to what choice of action we must or can take, as such are the phobias and fears of trepidation that also gives way to the rise of hope, so that we may come face to face with destiny.

As with each new day comes a new beginning, and with each new beginning comes new hopes and new expectations, as there are also new obstacles and challenges to overcome, as such is the dawning of life, to present to us all, such necessary and redeemable qualities within the observations of our lives, for to have hope, is to look up toward the heavens, and to quietly and silently know, that within this observation, that the sky or indeed the heavens, are still upheld by the forces of nature, that govern from above albeit much to our amazement and expectations, and that life is ordinarily and justly so, as we in our appreciation cannot always see beyond that which is so perfectly bound and set in motion with us in this universe, as we simply learn to believe and accept that this is the way of our living and all things besides us, as we are within all that has become created and laid out before us.

And yet with this new day dawning, if not for us to simply wake up and to use our hopes, and our aspirations to ascend beyond the obvious point of creation, and to apply our spiritual nature and positive will of motivation toward it, and it toward us upon reflection, as in our overcoming and prevailing, within its and our own destiny and deliverance, as such is also our descent to take warmth and courage, and comfort and refuge, when we lay down to take rest and sleep beneath the Moon and the Stars above, is also to take strength and peace of mind, in the hope and the understanding that a new day beginning, and a new dawning shall be presented to us once again, as this is the way of the life that we have come to know it, within our own divine ability and acceptance of it.

As much as life is and can very much be a challenge, it also appears to state, that there is a thread of universal commonality running through the whole of creation no matter what we profess to live and abide by as human beings, as for me the basis of these requirements that extend from this commonality is food, shelter, clothing, companionship, and a sense of connection or clarity derived from self awareness, that is not to say that there is not much more for broad scope beyond this basic measure and requirement that puts us all on an equal footing with one another, no matter where we inhabit or dwell in the world.

And so what and where are we permitted upon this universal basis, to gravitate towards, or indeed to excel to, in order to fulfill our existential experiences and engage with our full potential, as many of us in our progression towards modernity, would indeed interpretate this kind of idea or philosophy, depending upon which part of the world we lived in or inhabited, as being very much viewed differently realized upon that same broad basis, which also brings me to ask, and to question, and to examine this brave new world within this context, or indeed as some would profess to say or mention, within this new world order, or new world system, as there is much to address and to consider for all concerned.

For once we have evolved and grown and matured away from our basic needs and requirements, it would also appear that many of us who have indeed excelled, or concluded in the context of a post-modernistic era of environment or society, to have almost achieved something, which is of a value, or at least on a par with something that is equally attributed, to that of a spiritual level of attainment, or indeed enlightenment, but when we address the cost of such achievement, we also begin to see that we are still somewhat grounded in our best efforts by this basic requirement, which is to achieve, acquire, and survive at will, and to endure, and to live, and to abide by such new discoveries of achievements.

As even in this progress and achievement of what we would wish, or presume to call a new world, how do we fairly address or balance, or differentiate between those of us who are yet to grasp the basis of this understanding that is required for us to excel, or indeed for us to fly, or indeed to reach the highest spiritual level of attainment of understanding, of being, doing, and knowing, as in realizing that indeed not many of us could have, or would have had the opportunity, or indeed the privilege, of exercising such expressions of freedom in our new found world.

As some of us are fundamentally held by the very conventions of what is required upon this, a basic level of our independence, maintenance, and survival, to regulate and maintain the simplicity of ourselves, and yet once we have experienced and entertained this new idea inside such a concept, our first response is how should we, or what should we do in order to engage with one another, to bring about its universality as a basic principle and as a must for all concerned, and how can it be any good for us, if indeed we all profoundly have separate agendas, or different ideals, as to what should, or could take precedence over the basic and fundamental needs to live out our lives, when food, and shelter, and clothing, and companionship, and a sense of self, or a clarity of awareness is needed at the very heart of what it is, to not only be, but remain humane.

As for the background, or indeed the backdrop, and the combining and dedicated efforts, that it has taken me as a writer to come to arrive at within this story of the Angel Babies, and of course the time that it has taken for me, to construct, and to collate the necessary, and if I may say worthy and worthwhile aspects, for this particular body of work to become written and completed within the trilogy of the Angel Babies, I would very much like just like to inform the readership, that upon exploration and construction of this body of work, that I myself as a person, have experienced several variables of conversions upon my spiritual and emotional being, upon the instruction and initiation of bringing the series of these books into the light.

For had I not been introduced into the many schools of thought and allied faiths of Christianity, Islam, Hare Krsna, Hindu, Buddhism, Dao and Shinto, that it may never have transpired or surmounted, or indeed would have been very much an arduous and challenging task, to find the right motivation for the narrative, very much needed and applied, with which to find and devise the relative inspiration, and ideas explored and written within the context and narrative of the characters and the storyline that I have presented to you as an author.

*~ **Clive Alando Taylor***

REFERENCE

Empyrean - (Heaven/Angelic Dwelling Place)
Haven - (Hope)
Hark the Herald - (The Listening Angel)
Angel Nephi - (Nephilim)
Simeon - (The Protecting Angel)
Stefan - (The Angel Of Love)
Ophlyn - (The Fallen Angel)
Papiosa - Father Of Anahita / Character Depicting Good and Evil)
Leoine - Mother Of Anahita / (Bastion & Sentient)
Men Shen - **(Taoist Interpretation meaning
/ Guardians of the Door)**
Angel Of Justice - (figuratively)
Anahita - (Earth Mother)
Selah - (Earth Mother)
Kali Ma - (Hindu Supreme Goddess or Black Earth Mother)
Gabriel - (Archangel)
Michael - (Archangel)
Raguel - (Archangel)
Raphael - (Archangel)
Remiel - (Archangel)
Uriel - (Archangel)
Zerachiel - (Archangel)
Nejeru - (New Jerusalem)
Golden Dawn - (The Future)
(Emanations Of God)
Monad the **One** / **Bythos** the **Aeon** / **Proarkhe** the **Arkhe**
Throne Of God - (Emerald Green/Ophanim)

~*~

Definitive
Angelus Domini
*A **Tao.House** Product/**Angel***
Babies Immortality VII
*LOVE*BELOVED *LOVE*
Valentine Fountain of Love Ministry
Info contact: ***tao.house@live.co.uk***
Copyright: Clive Alando Taylor 2016

~*~

Printed in the United States
By Bookmasters